Two College Friends

Two College Friends

Frederick W. Loring

MINT EDITIONS

Two College Friends was first published in 1871.

This edition published by Mint Editions 2021.

ISBN 9781513218366 | E-ISBN 9781513217369

Published by Mint Editions®

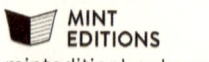
MINT EDITIONS

minteditionbooks.com

Publishing Director: Jennifer Newens
Design & Production: Rachel Lopez Metzger
Project Manager: Micaela Clark
Typesetting: Westchester Publishing Services

"At dawn," he said, "I bid them all farewell,
To go where bugles blow and rifles gleam."
And with the waking thought asleep he fell,
And wandered into dream.

A great hot plain from lake to ocean spread,
Through it a level river slowly drawn:
He moved with a vast crowd, and at its head
Streamed banners like the dawn.

Then came a blinding flash, a deafening roar,
And dissonant cries of terror and dismay;
Blood trickled down the river's reedy shore,
And with the dead he lay.

The morn broke in upon his solemn dream,
And still with steady pulse and deepening eye,
"Where bugles call," he said, "and rifles gleam,
I follow, though I die."

Contents

I

The Lecture on Domestic Arts

"'At dawn,' he said, 'I bid them all farewell,
To go where bugles blow and rifles gleam;'
And with the waking thought asleep he fell,
And wandered into dream."

It was quarter after two in the afternoon, and the Professor was sitting at his desk, engaged in arranging the notes of his lecture, when there came a knock on the door.

"Come in," said the Professor. "Ah, Ned! is it you?" This to a graceful boy of twenty, who entered the room.

"Yes, it is Ned," said the boy; "and he particularly wishes to see you for a few minutes."

"Every moment is precious," said the Professor, "until my lecture is in order. What is the matter? Are you in trouble?"

"Yes," said Ned, "I am in trouble."

"Then let me read to you," said the Professor, "the concluding paragraph of my lecture on Domestic Arts."

"Oh, don't!" said Ned; "I really am in trouble."

"Are you the insulter or the insulted, this time?" asked the Professor.

"Neither," said Ned, shortly; "and I'm not in trouble on my own account."

"Ah!" said the Professor; "then you have got into some difficulty in your explorations in low life; or you have spent more than your income; or it's the perpetual Tom."

"It's the perpetual Tom," said Ned.

"I supposed so," observed the Professor. "What has that youth been doing now? Drinking, swearing, gambling, bad company, theft, murder?—out with it! I am prepared for anything, from the expression of your face; for anything, that is to say, except my lecture on Domestic Arts, which comes at three."

"Well, if you choose to make fun of me," said Ned, "I can go; but I thought you would advise me."

"And so I will, you ridiculous creature, when you need it," said the Professor; "only at such times you generally act for yourself. But, come; my advice and sympathy are yours; so what has Tom done?"

"He has fallen in love," said Ned.

"Oh, no!" said the Professor.

"Yes, sir," repeated Ned, more firmly, "he has fallen in love."

"'Tis the way of all flesh," said the Professor; "but I don't think Tom can fall in love. He never even dislikes anyone without a cause."

"That's all very well, sir," said Ned; "but when a fellow has a girl's picture, and looks at it when he thinks he isn't watched; and when he receives notes, and keeps them, instead of throwing them around, as usual; and when he takes to being blue,—what do you say?"

"Please state your propositions separately," said the Professor, "and I will endeavor to form an opinion. When a fellow has a girl's picture,— what was the rest?"

"I wish you wouldn't make fun of me," said Ned.

"Well, in Heaven's name, what is there to trouble you, if Tom is in love?" asked the Professor.

"Because he hasn't told me," said Ned.

"Oh! you are jealous then," rejoined the Professor. "You are the most selfish person, for one who is so generous, that I have ever seen. You are morbid upon the subject of Tom, I believe."

"Well, look here," said Ned; "I have neither father nor mother; I have no one except Tom. I care more for him than for anyone else in the world, as you know; but you never will know how much I care for him; and it does seem hard that he should shut me out of his confidence when I have done nothing to forfeit it. There's some girl at the bottom of all this. He and that big Western friend of his, the Blush Rose, whom I never liked, have been off together two or three times; and, as I say, Tom has got this picture; and the Blush Rose knows it, and knows who she is. I've seen them looking at it, and admiring it. I'm afraid, from Tom's not telling me about it, that he's doing something out of the way."

"In that case," said the Professor, "you had better let me read you the closing paragraph of my lecture on Domestic Arts."

"No, I thank you," said Ned; "I shall have to hear it, anyway, this afternoon."

"So you will," said the Professor; "and, by the way, I shall give you a private if you behave today as you did in my last lecture. I have told your class-tutor to warn you."

FREDERICK W. LORING

"Well, that is pleasant," said Ned.

"I meant it to be," replied the Professor. "Goodbye. I may call at your room tonight,—to see Tom."

And, as Ned was heard going down the stairs, the Professor, seeing that he had still twenty-five minutes to spare, took his lecture, and sat down before the fire, which flickered slightly, and just served to destroy the dampness of that April day.

II

The Picture Over the Fireplace

Whether the Professor would have made any alterations or amendments in his lecture, it is difficult to say; that he did not is due to the fact that his eye fell upon a little photograph, which hung over his fireplace. As he sits there, thinking over what Ned has told him, and laughing at the idea of Tom's being really in love, he gazes on this little photograph, and smiles. The Professor has one or two real art treasures, but nothing that he values quite as much as this fading picture. This is the only copy in existence; and this hangs there, and will hang there until the Professor dies. How well he remembers the morning when the two boys, whom he loves so well, rushed into his room, and left it there! As he looks at it now, there is an expression of tenderness on his plain but strongly cut features that would greatly astonish those of his pupils who only know him as a crusty instructor.

The Professor is somewhat crusty, it must be owned. It is, however, an acquired and not a natural crustiness. Cause, the fact that at thirty years of age he discovered that he cared more for a certain Miss Spencer than for all the world beside. On intimating this fact to her, she told him that she should always value his friendship; and that she hoped soon to introduce to him her cousin Hugh, "who is," she added quietly, "to become my husband." After this the Professor withdrew almost entirely from society, and plunged deeper and deeper into study. Before many years his reputation was cosmopolitan, his head bald, and his life a matter of routine. Boys came and went; and at intervals he repeated before them much of what he knew. It is to these two boys, of whom he thinks now, as he gazes on the picture over the mantel, that he owes his rescue from this lethargic life.

What does he see in the picture? He sees behind a chair, in which a boy is sitting, another boy with soft, curling brown hair, deep blue eyes, and dazzling complexion. His features are delicately cut; but the especial beauty of his face is the brilliancy of color in his hair, eyes, and complexion. There is the freshness of youth on his features; and his whole attitude, as he leans over his companion, is full of that quaint grace of boyish tenderness so indefinable and so transitory. The boy in the chair has a face full of strength and weakness. The photograph makes him appear the more striking of the two, though the less handsome. The sunny sweetness of the first face, though it never alters, never becomes wearisome; but the second face is now all love, now disfigured by scorn and hatred, now full of intellect, and glowing with animation, now sullen and morose. The complexion is olive, the eyes brown, the lips strongly cut, yet so mobile as to be capable of every variety of earnest and sneering expression. The face is always, in all its varying phases, the face of one who is not dissatisfied but unsatisfied. This is what the Professor sees, as the firelight throws its glimmer over the room, making grotesque shadows waver fitfully on the pictures and books around him, as well as on the heavy curtains that hide the rays of afternoon light which struggle through the leafy boughs of the old elms in the yard without.

As the Professor sits there thinking, he seems to recall again the first visit of Tom and Ned to his room. Tom is a lovely boy,—the original of the standing figure in the photograph; and the Professor had been attracted by his face once or twice when he had met him in the yard, soon after his entrance into college. Still he is surprised, one evening, when he hears a knock at his door, and this Freshman enters half shyly. The Professor asks him to be seated, and then looks at him inquiringly.

"I was awfully homesick," says Tom, with perfect trustfulness; "and mother told me that you were once a very dear friend of hers; so I thought I would come up and see you." The Professor is bewildered. Still he is a gentleman; so he smiles, and says to Tom:—

"Pray be seated. Your mother is well, I trust."

"Oh, yes!" says Tom. "Perhaps, as she hasn't seen you since before I was born, I ought to have said who she was. Her name was Spencer."

The Professor turns quickly. Tom proceeds with entire unconsciousness:—

"She often speaks of you, sir, and always in a way that has made me want to know you."

"I am very glad, Tom," said the Professor. "You must excuse my calling you by your first name; but then you are the son of—your mother."

Anyone but Tom, who never noticed anything, would have seen here that the Professor's manner was peculiar. But Tom is always so brightly ignorant of what is before his eyes, that the Professor recovers his self-possession, and says calmly:—

"And your mother is well, I hope?"

"Oh, yes!" said Tom; "very well, but a little sad at my leaving home. She is very fond of me, sir."

"Strange fact!" said the Professor, dryly. "And I see that you are equally fond of her. I am not given to moralizing; but I think that college life will not decay you, if you don't forget how much you are to your mother,—how unhappy you can make her."

"Forget her?" said Tom; "not I! When I am at home, I make love to her all the time."

"Then," said the Professor, "it is well that you have left home; for it will soon be time for you to make love to someone else."

As the Professor makes this observation, there is another knock at the door, and Ned enters. Who is Ned? Ned is the original of the sitting figure in the little picture over the fireplace. He is despotic in character, and has therefore many sincere friends and enemies. He is fearless when indignant, and is indignant easily. He is not handsome as Tom is,—for Tom's beauty charms you immediately, and the charm is never broken; but he has a curious grace and fascination of manner when he is not perverse; but then, he often is perverse.

The Professor cannot tell whether he likes Ned, or not. He has been giving Ned private tuition, to fit him for college, for nearly a year. All their acquaintance hitherto has been one of business, all their conversation confined to an occasional dry remark on either side. Now, when their contract is fulfilled, the Professor cannot imagine why Ned should take advantage of his general invitation, and visit him. Still he asks Ned to be seated, and then enters into conversation with him.

Ned talks. His keen eye has noted everything ludicrous and everything interesting among his instructors, among his classmates, among all the persons and things with which college life has brought him in contact. He is full of animation; he tells stories, all of which have a point; he sparkles with wit, which is none the less brilliant for having a certain boyish freshness about it. All this is a new revelation to the Professor. He laughs, and in his turn becomes entertaining; and, finally, going to his sideboard, produces three quaint glasses, which he fills with some of that rare and wonderful old Madeira, which many of his acquaintances have heard of, but which few have ever seen.

Tom, in the mean time, sits listening, radiant with enjoyment, with the firelight tinting his lovely face. "Such a jolly old fellow as this Professor is!" he says to himself; "and such a being as Ned!" He is happier than he has been since he left home; and he wishes his mother could look in upon them now; and he drains his glass to her health. He is puzzled because Ned will address his remarks only to the Professor, and seems shy whenever he speaks. Finally, conscious that it is growing late, he bids the Professor farewell, and Ned rises to accompany him. The Professor says then, with a courteous and quiet dignity:—

"Tom, you must give my regards to your mother, when you write. Tell her that her boy will be always an object of especial interest to her old friend." Then, turning to Ned, the Professor adds, as Tom disappears in the entry:—

"I have to thank you for a very pleasant evening. You will come again, my boy, will you not? Why have you never before shown me what you really are?"

"It wasn't for you, sir," said Ned, with a certain frankness that was not discourteous. "It was for Tom, sir; though I like you, and hope we shall be friends. But the moment I saw Tom, I felt drawn towards him; and, as I saw him come up here, I felt that here was a chance to get acquainted with him. Goodnight, sir."

And Ned joined Tom at the foot of the stairs, leaving the Professor in a state of complete bewilderment. The Professor laughs now, as he recalls that evening, and looks again at the picture over the fireplace.

"They are an interesting pair,—a sunbeam and a volcano," he says; and, throwing on his cloak, just as the bell begins to ring, he starts for his lecture-room.

III

HE MOVED WITH A VAST CROWD

It was just after supper; and the Professor, with his thoughts still occupied by Tom and Ned, walked slowly toward his room through the dimly-lighted yard, where the twilight was half dispelled by the gleams of gas-light that stole from the windows around. He sauntered along, enjoying the sweet spring air of the evening, and touching his hat to one boy after another until he came by Ned's entry, when he turned, and took his way to the room of his boys. He had stopped, as he passed through the square, for his paper, and had noticed that a crowd seemed to be eagerly and excitedly discussing the news of the evening around the post-office. Pausing an instant in the entry to look at his paper, before ascending the stairs, his eye fell on an announcement which caused him to utter an exclamation of surprise; and he rushed eagerly into the room, with the words:—

"Boys, have you heard the news?"

Ned turned from the glass, where he was tying his cravat, and Tom raised himself from his lounge; but before either of them had an opportunity to answer, the Professor said:—

"There has been a quarrel here. Now, boys, I must know all about it. See, I'm going to spring the lock, and have you clear your minds at once."

"There's nothing to clear," said Tom.

"Speak for yourself, if you please," said the Professor. "You may not have a mind at all; but I know that Ned has, to a limited extent. Doubtless you are both wrong; so let me see which will be gentleman enough to apologize first. Come, boys, this matter must be set right. 'Let not the sun go down upon your wrath' is one of the best pieces of advice ever given."

"It is after sunset now," said Ned; "and we are not both wrong. I am right."

"Cheerful self-confidence," said the Professor. "Please let me understand the cause of wrath."

"Simply because I object to the Blush Rose," said Ned. "I say that he has come between us."

     FREDERICK W. LORING

"And I say"—broke in Tom.

"Hush, Tom!" said the Professor, "until Ned has finished."

"I have nothing more to say," said Ned, "except that Tom must, once for all, choose between us."

"Very well," said Tom; "as you please; only, while I don't care for any fellow as I do for you, I'm not going to submit to dictation."

"You're entangled with some woman, through Blodgett," said Ned. "He's a nice associate for a gentleman, he is."

"I entangled with a woman!" repeated Tom. "Why, Ned! you're crazy."

"Whose picture is it that you are carrying?" asked Ned.

"Oh, thunder!" said Tom; "is that what all this row is about?"

"I suppose you've fallen in love, and in Junior year too!" continued Ned, wrathfully and contemptuously.

"Juniors have done such things before," observed the Professor.

"Fallen in love!" said Tom; "as if I'd do that! Look here, old fellow, if you knew about that picture, you'd ask my pardon."

"Well, as I don't, I shan't," said Ned.

"Come, boys," said the Professor, "this ridiculous quarrel, worthy only of a couple of little children, has gone quite far enough. Ned, I think you are petulant and absurd; but if you will go out for a few minutes, and take a short walk, Tom will unbosom himself to me, I am sure."

"Well, I call that cheek, to turn a man out of his own room," said Ned.

"Correct that sentence, please, Ned," said the Professor. "You would call it cheek if it were not done by a member of the Faculty. There, be off with you. And now, Tom, tell your story."

"I haven't any," said Tom; "only Ned is in one of his moods."

"Then you are not in love," said the Professor.

"Why, no!" said Tom, "how could I be?"

"I don't know," replied the Professor; "but people are sometimes. And have you a secret connected with that fat, red-faced brute, Blodgett, whom you call the Blush Rose?"

"Well, yes," said Tom: "it's about a photograph."

"Let us see this photograph," said the Professor. "Explain!"

"Why, it's a surprise for Ned, don't you see?" said Tom. "It's the proof picture of me in the last theatricals. See, there I am as Marton, the Pride of the Market."

"What a mistake nature made about your sex, Tom!" said the Professor. "You dear little peasant girl, put yourself away directly; and now take my advice: show it to Ned; it will make him ashamed of his folly, and will prevent any further angry words between you. It is hard to quarrel, and so you will think some day, though now you find it so easy. There, put it away; for I hear Ned's footsteps on the stairs! Come in, Ned! Why! what has happened?"

For Ned, standing in the open door-way, his perverse moodiness all gone, wore an expression the Professor had never seen before.

"Happened!" said Ned. "Something to live for, something to die for. We know now that we have a country. Haven't you heard the news?"

"Dear me!" said the Professor, "that's what I came to tell you; but your quarrel drove it out of my head."

"How could anything else come into your head?" said Ned.

"Tell me what it is," asked Tom, impatiently.

"The President has called the people to arms, to aid him in saving the country," said Ned, fairly glowing as he spoke.

"Yes," said the Professor, "is it not grand to think that we are aroused at last?"

"Well," said Ned, "I have still more to tell you. I have enlisted."

There was a pause of a few moments; then the Professor grasped Ned's hand, and said simply:—

"My noble boy!"

"What do you say, Tom?" asked Ned.

"I'm going with you, old fellow," said Tom; and he threw his arm over Ned's shoulder, and smiled at the Professor.

FREDERICK W. LORING

IV

Ned's Note-Book

It is well that I formed the habit of keeping a note-book sometime ago. How interesting what I am now writing will be to my wife and children in years to come, when I sit before my own fire, in my own house! The college chronicle of funny adventures and curious stories that my note-book has previously contained is suspended for a time; and I am thinking of matters of life and death now. Well, it is splendid to have a life to lose; and the thought of death, in this cause, has a grand, awful thrill in it, that drives away all the former terror death has possessed for me. These remarks are intended as an opening of my war note-book. Here am I, just twenty-one, and a captain,—a whole captain. It is absurd; no, it isn't. Col. Burke is raising a regiment. He has as much superfluity about him as an iron nail has, and no more. He was introduced to me about a week ago, and was told about my visits to the people around Crescent Court. People will make me out a philanthropist, which I am not; for I despise most people I know, though the lower classes are quite interesting, but dirty. I never talked religion to any of those creatures in my life. I have given them very little in charity; but I have listened to what they say as I would to my own classmates; and, having talked with them at the North End, I have bowed to them at the West End. In a word, I have carried *les convenances* into Richmond Street, and have not electioneered. Result, I have some influence, which is useless, except in keeping me clear of pickpockets. So the colonel would have me raise a company. I laughed at the idea, but consented to try; and here are over fifty recruits already. I told them that I had about as much to learn as any of them, and agreed to have the captain elected by vote, myself becoming a private. I should have been very much disgusted if they had taken me at my word; but they didn't. So I am a captain; but my lieutenants are still to be found.

Tom is full of patriotism. I never can tell how deeply a sentiment enters his mind; but he is fretting terribly about going with me. How I wish he could! but his father very sensibly advises him to wait a year longer, till he is through at Harvard; and his mother is in great distress at the idea of his leaving her. The Professor is non-committal on the subject.

THIS MORNING ENTERED JANE ELLEN Bingley to the recruiting office, where I was receiving enlistments. Jane Ellen is limp in appearance, but energetic in character. Her bonnet was wine-colored velvet; her shawl draggled green, with a habit of falling off her shoulders as she talked; and her gown was calico. By the bonnet I recognized her. She is the chief attraction at one of the North Street dance-houses, and entertains an admiration for me of which I am utterly undeserving. I have so often declined in forcible language to dance with her, that I did not suppose she could feel pleasantly toward me; but she came forward and said:—

"Here's my man!"

Her man was a stout fellow, rather stupid-looking, with a dyed mustache. Jane Ellen herself is really very pretty, and might possibly reform, if she was sent away from here. Reformation, when possible, is only possible through removal. So Jane Ellen having presented her man, I said briefly:—

"What of it?"

Thereupon Jane Ellen explained that her man wished to enlist, and that she wished him to come under me, as she knew I'd be a good captain to the poor boy. Sensible of the compliment, I suggested to Jane Ellen the propriety of marrying him first. In that way I explained to her he would send her his salary (I could not say wages, Jane Ellen being American); he would have some object for working his way up from the ranks; and he would have a home to think of, when away, wounded, sick, or expecting to die. All these things would benefit him greatly. I regret to say that Michael appeared more affected than Jane Ellen at the pictures I drew. Jane Ellen's answer, which only came after considerable reflection, was, to say the least, peculiar.

"I never expected to live to be a married woman," she remarked; "and it's a queer home I'd be able to make for anybody. However, it may do Mike good; so I'll do it. So, Mike, I'll marry you right off, and endeavor to be a decent woman,—until you come back from the war again"; which last clause was prudently added.

ANOTHER QUARREL WITH TOM; AND this time the Professor admits that I am right. Tom begs me to write, and solicit his parents' consent; and I won't do it; so Tom sulks,—that is the only word,—and will not be appeased.

He even declares that I wish to get rid of him, when it will almost break my heart to go without him. If that boy only knew what he was to me, who am without father, mother, or family of my own, and with almost no friends, except the Professor! However, for the same reason that I have never yet visited him at his house, because I did not wish to have our attachment or my character analyzed or criticised by his parents, I will not say a word now. I believe it will do him good to go; for I know the thought of going has done me good.

The Professor has a plan, he says, and wishes me to be at home tonight, so that he can tell it to me.

THE PROFESSOR HAS TOLD ME a great deal more than he has actually said. I know now why he cares so much for Tom; and I should like to see Tom's mother. I wonder if a woman will ever change my life; and I wonder if I shall ever care for any woman as much as I do for Tom. The Professor says that Tom must go; that he is fretting himself sick now, and that it will develop his manliness of character. He thinks I am right in not interfering, however, and says that he is going to try what he can do. Dear old fellow! His face flushed, and he gave a curious sort of gulp, as he said:—

"She always respected me; and I think she would let Tom go, if I advised her to do so."

"Then shall you write to her?" I asked.

"No, Ned," he said; "I shall go and visit her, and start tomorrow. The first time in twenty years,—dear me, the first time in twenty years! How old I am getting to be!"

I knew what he meant; and I honored his pluck. I should sort of like to be in love myself; but I am half afraid to think about it. Oh, well! there will be plenty of time when the war is over. The Professor is to start tomorrow; and Tom is not to know about it.

MY FIRST LIEUTENANT IS A treasure. His name is Murphy; and he is a retired rough, by profession, but he has splendid stuff in him. Our acquaintance had a peculiar beginning. I was drilling a squad of men, and not succeeding very well in what I was about, when this giant loafed in, and began to make a disturbance. I looked at him, and saw that remonstrance would be in vain; so I knocked him down, seeing my opportunity to do so effectively. My men laughed. The giant raised himself in astonishment.

"You can't do that again," said he. Another laugh from the chorus.

"I know it," said I Still another laugh.

"I could just walk through you in two minutes," he growled, with an oath.

"I believe you," said I; "and I shall give you a chance to, if you don't keep quiet."

He kept quiet for a time. Then, while I was trying some manœuvre, he came up and said, quite politely:—

"Perhaps I can help you."

"Thanks," said I; "do you know anything about it?" Then Murphy informed me that he had been in several places where there had been fighting; and I saw he was far my superior in many respects. So, when I got him to enlist, and found that he was thoroughly interested, and that the men liked him with a feeling of fellowship that they will never have for me, I hope, I talked with the colonel about making him my first lieutenant; and it is now a *fait accompli*. Murphy's delight and gratitude at receiving his commission knew no bounds; and several of his cousins enlisted immediately. He has now a sense of personal devotion to me that will help me greatly. Dear me, how old and mature and self-reliant I am growing! and, three weeks ago, I was such a baby! Murphy is the second largest and second strongest man of us all. The largest is a large-eyed, half-crazy clairvoyant, gentle as a dove, and strong as an ox. I found him weeping the other day; and, somewhat disgusted, as well as astonished, asked the cause. Result was, that he said he wept about me. I was not to die in battle, nor in sickness, but was to meet with a dishonorable death for a dishonorable action. Tom and Murphy were furious; but I couldn't be before the two or three men who heard it; so I treated the affair as a good joke. The boys call this fellow Mooney; which name is appropriate certainly. Tom has been in two or three times to drill. He studies Hardee incessantly; practises by himself all that he can, and would form himself into a whole squad, and drill himself, if it were possible. He is even getting into the way of planning battles and movements, and is perfectly wild at each report in the newspapers. I never saw him in such a state before, over anything. His lessons must be suffering in consequence; and I don't dare to think of the number of times he has cut prayers.

HURRAH! I WISH PENCIL AND paper could yell with joy; and then a fearful noise would issue from this note-book!

The Professor has sent me by telegraph the announcement that Tom is to go with me. It is brief; but I have read it with delight a dozen times:—

FREDERICK W. LORING

"All Right! Please Send Him Home Immediately!"

I know of nothing which has ever given me more pleasure than those seven words. Tom has gone off in the most remarkably vague state of mind; and I am going to see my colonel this evening, to find out whether his youth (though, as he is not quite two years younger than myself, perhaps I should say our youth) will unfit him for the position of second lieutenant. Anyway, he's going; and that's enough to make me happy for the rest of the war. The only thing that troubles me is Mooney's prediction, which keeps ringing in my ears. I am not to die in battle, nor by sickness, but to receive a dishonorable death for a dishonorable action. I don't care for the death so much; but I do pray to God, that, while I am in my country's holy service at least, I may not soil my soul. What a sentence! Well, I'm safe in knowing that no one but myself will ever see this note-book.

V

Correspondence

1

My Dear Tom

This letter will reach you after you have been at home a day; and you must leave home as soon as you receive it, to join my company. Our colonel is splendid,—grim and grizzled, and the nerve of a steam-engine. I told him about you, and said I wanted you as second lieutenant. He asked how much you knew; and I said, "Little enough, but more than any other of my vagabonds,—God bless them!" Then I told him about your study of Hardee; and he laughed, but asked me anxiously what you thought of Hardee. I forget what I said; but I know your opinion satisfied him perfectly; for he said that your youth was your greatest disqualification. Then I said that the rough set of my company needed the influence of an acknowledged gentleman, as well as the fellow-feeling and sympathy which that rough Murphy gives them. He agreed to that. Then he spoke of the value, in any rank of life, of a university education;—he hasn't been through Harvard, you see;—and I agree with him. Then, when he heard who was your father, and who was your mother, he smiled, and said he believed in blood. I agreed again with him, and expressed the opinion that no one could get along very well without it. Moreover, I said, that, if you did not come as an officer, the whole company would become insubordinate; for you always had your own way with me; and it would not do for a private to control his captain. He laughed; but you are sure of your position, if you come on at once. We are not a swell regiment, Tom; but my sword-belt and sash are stunning, for all that. You must begin work at once. And, Tom, you must feel an interest in Murphy. It will do him good; and, through him, the men. He dined with me today, and made an attempt to eat with his fork instead of his knife, which was tolerably successful. He is a little uneasy about meeting you, being sensible of a certain lack of polish in his manner; but with you as the positive pole, and I as the negative, we shall have him duly magnetized in time.

I have been out to Cambridge, to see about destroying our old room; but I could not do it. I sat down and cried like a towel, or a sponge; I couldn't help it. The goody had profited by your absence to leave everything out of order; for which I thanked her in my soul. The pictures that I hated, and the pictures that you didn't like, hung on the walls; your dressing-gown was in your chair; the globe in which our departed goldfish once resided was still swinging at the window; and everything seemed like a dream of the past to me. Well, I should have been a brute if I hadn't felt a little touched.

O Tom! you've forgotten to return "Roderick Random" to the library; and Sibley will come down on you for a nice lot of fines, see if he don't.

But I was going to tell you about our room. Bob Lennox, who is rooming outside, you know, wants to come in as tenant during our absence, so that we can have everything just as it always has been, when we come back by next class-day; by which time, I am quite sure, the war will be ended; so I agreed to his proposition, subject to your objection, of course.

I thought, since your educational advantages impressed the colonel, that a copy of the last rank-list might work in your favor; but I decided, finally, that it would require too much explanation. In the same way I was thinking of getting you a certificate of moral character from Dr. Peabody, but was not sure that he had forgotten you sufficiently.

If you wish to secure your position, you must be here by Friday night. My love to the Professor, and sincere regards to your father and mother.

In haste, but, as ever,
your friend,
NED

2

MY DEAR OLD NED

Your letter was just like you, cross old devil that you are! I'm coming, old horse; so write my name down on your parchment immediately. The Professor starts this noon, and says he will wait over a train for me in Endeston, where he wants to make a visit this afternoon; so that I shall start tomorrow morning, and meet him there. Mother says it's because he has so much delicacy of feeling that he doesn't want to see our parting; and, by Jove! Ned, it's going to be hard. She doesn't say much; but I know how she suffers; and it makes me almost feel as though I was wrong to go. I'll bet I'll have a handsomer sash than you will, after all. Mother wants me to give you the enclosed letter, which seems mysterious to me; still I obey. I am in a great hurry, so can't write anymore, but shall be with you on Friday.

Yours,

TOM

3

MY DEAR NED,

For though I have never yet had the pleasure of seeing you at our house, I still feel as though I knew you, Tom has said so much to me of you, and has shown so much more than he has said. I have felt very thankful that you were his friend; and now that this terrible and dreadful parting is to separate me from my only child, I am glad that you are to be with him. I know the cause that calls him, and I feel that it is better for him to go than to stay; but, though I say yes, I say it with an agony beyond your comprehension. I want your promise that you will not leave Tom during the time that your country may need you; that you will suffer nothing but death to separate you; that you will refuse promotion and honor, if it is to part you from him; that you will stay by his side in the progress of the battles that may come. It is through your influence that he goes; I must look to you for his safety. So make me this promise; and, in return, what can I give? what can I say? This only: that my house shall be your home; and that I shall feel as if I had two sons instead of one.

VI

One Year After

"A great hot plain from sea to mountain spread;
Through it a level river slowly drawn:
He moved with a vast crowd, and at its head
Streamed banners like the dawn."

A bare room, the dead whiteness of whose plastered wall is only relieved by a coarsely colored print of the Virgin Mary in blue and scarlet, which hangs in a dingy gilt frame on the wall at the head of the bed. A crack in the glass has relieved the features of the Virgin of their ordinary expression of insipidity, but has substituted therefor a look of malevolence quite unpleasant to see. Fortunately for the man who lies, heavily sleeping, upon the pallet bed, this picture is not where his eyes can rest upon it. Beside the bed are two little stools, which constitute all the furniture of the room, and, indeed, all that it is well capable of containing; for so cramped and narrow are its dimensions, that it seems to be scarcely more than a closet with a window in it. Through the half-open door-way, however, can be seen long lines of beds, with the quiet figures of nurses and physicians passing back and forth through the ward.

Two people entered carefully and noiselessly through the open door-way,—one evidently an army physician; the other, in a captain's uniform now, was Tom, bronzed and sunburnt, but the same careless, light-hearted boy as when he left Cambridge one year before. There was a look of anxiety on his face now, however, as he bent over the sleeping figure and asked:—

"How is he today, doctor?"

"Improving fast, captain," was the reply. "His sleep is splendid,—just what I've been hoping for. If he wakes peacefully, and is conscious, he is likely to be all right again before long; and I shouldn't wonder if he could rejoin his regiment in a week or ten days."

"Thank Heaven!" said Tom.

"And his physique," said the doctor. "This colonel of yours is a tough fellow, and a brave man; yet, if he should die tomorrow, I should simply put down his name, and never think of him again. My note-book is full of dead men's names,—just a mention and nothing more. Oh! by the way, a gentleman called here for you yesterday afternoon, and said he would come again this morning. Here is his card."

"Why," cried Tom, "it is the Professor. See that he is shown up to me when he comes, won't you?"

"Oh, certainly! I'll attend to that," said the doctor, and he rushed softly away.

Tom sat down by the side of the bed, and looked at his friend's face. It had changed greatly, much more than his, since they left Cambridge. The forehead was marked now with heavy lines, and the full beard made it seem like the countenance of a man of forty. So old can even a boy grow in a year. Ned had trained himself, with great effort, to unquestioning obedience. His criticism had been only upon those to whom he gave his orders, and he had struggled not to form an opinion on those to whom his obedience was due; thus he had become an admirable officer. Tom sat there looking at Ned, and thinking, thinking, he could scarcely tell of what, until he felt a hand touch his shoulder. He turned and saw the Professor, and fairly hugged him in his delight.

"So I have found you at last, Tom," said the Professor.

"Just think, sir," said Tom; "it is a year now since I have seen you."

"And the end seems as far off as ever," said the Professor.

"Don't say that," said Tom, "because sometimes, you know, I have to try very hard not to think so myself."

"Ah!" said the Professor, "you are still the same, I see, and I am the same; and Ned,—is this Ned?"

"Yes, poor fellow," said Tom; "he has been sick for nearly ten days."

"But how came you to be with him?" asked the Professor. "Why are you not with your regiment?"

"Sit down," said Tom, "and I'll tell you; but don't speak too loud, on his account, you know!"

"Among the wonderful effects of the war," said the Professor, in a didactic manner, "may be mentioned the fact that it has made Tom thoughtful and considerate. Well, go on!"

"That sounds just like you," said Tom. "Well, the explanation is simply this: that I had a leave of absence for a fortnight given me, and just at its beginning Ned was taken sick."

"So you remained here with him, and didn't go home?" asked the Professor.

"Of course," said Tom, simply. "I couldn't leave him after all we had been through together."

"What did your mother say?" asked the Professor. "Wasn't she disappointed?"

"Yes, she was disappointed," said Tom; "but she wrote and said that I was right. It was hard on Ned, and hard on me, and hard on her, especially as I haven't been home for a year. You see, in my last leave of absence, there was some of the worst fighting that we have been in, and it would have seemed cowardly if I had gone then."

"It is hard, Tom," said the Professor; "but you have done nobly. But if I stay here with Ned now, can't you run up North?"

"No," said Tom; "it's impossible. My leave of absence, you see, expires in two days, so that I shall have to give up going home at all for the present. I'm afraid now that Ned won't be well enough to satisfy me when I start for the front. He's been perfectly delirious, and yesterday the doctor said was the turning-point. If he only is conscious when he wakes from this sleep! Do you think he has changed?"

"Changed!" said the Professor; "he's not the same boy,—he's not a boy at all. What a developing agent this terrible war is!"

"And now you must tell me about Harvard," said Tom.

"Wait a minute," said the Professor. "I have one or two questions to ask you first. I want to hear about this new rebel general who is making such havoc with us."

"Stonewall Jackson, you mean," said Tom. "No one knows much about him; but Ned declares that he is, thus far, the most striking figure of the rebellion. Maliff, who says he knew him when he was in command at Fort Hamilton, before the war, showed us a picture of him, in which he looked simply prim and neat. The war has probably changed all that. I think we are all a little afraid of him, and hope to meet him in battle soon. Some of the men think he is a supernatural being."

"The Hibernian element, I suppose," said the Professor.

"Exactly," said Tom.

"And now tell me some more about yourselves," continued the Professor.

"Well, about ourselves," said Tom, "there is little to say. I am a captain, as you see; and Ned is a lieutenant-colonel, and commands our regiment,—or what there is left of it now. We might both have been promoted before this; but we were bound to stick together, and so we have, in all sorts of places too."

"I have heard," said the Professor, "how you have saved Ned's life."

"Nonsense!" said Tom. "He has done just as much for me. We are together, and we fight and quarrel, just as we did at Harvard; and, when the war is over, Ned insists that we are to go back to Cambridge for a year longer, so as to get our degrees; a plan which I don't altogether fancy."

"I do," said the Professor; "it will be delightful to me to have the opportunity of marking the misdemeanors of a colonel, and perhaps of even suspending a captain."

"That sounds just like you, and like old times," said Tom; "and now do please tell me all about Harvard."

"Yes," said Ned's voice feebly, from the bed, "please let us hear the Harvard news." And so the Professor began.

VII

NED'S NOTE-BOOK

Tom has gone, but the Professor is here still. I do not mean to stay long,—I shall rejoin my regiment in a day or two. In the mean time, I amuse myself, when the Professor is not here, by scribbling in my note-book and reading it over. Such a book as it is now! My own thoughts begin it; then, as we reach the battle-fields, I have not time to think, much less to put my thoughts in writing; then comes a record of deaths,—poor fellows, who wanted me to write to their homes. How curious that record is! Men whom I didn't care for grew heroic to me in those first days,—when death was a novelty,—and I am minute in my descriptions of them. Then, as the deaths become more and more frequent, my descriptions grow shorter, and I give a line only, even to those whom I really loved. It is strange reading, this note-book of mine!

Here is an item which I find in my note-book: "Quarrelled with Tom!" How we have fought, to be sure! I don't know what this quarrel was about, but I know how it ended. We didn't speak for two days, and then came another attack from that restless creature, Stonewall Jackson. It was such a lovely day,—fresh and spring-like, but it soon grew hot and dusty. Every once in a while a bullet would whiz past; I could hear the rumble of the artillery, and I was terribly thirsty. I didn't see Tom, but I knew he was near,—we always kept close together at such times;—still, if I had seen him, I wouldn't have spoken to him. My horse had been shot from under me, and I had cut open the head of the man who did it; it seems strange, now that it is all over, that I could do such a thing. Suddenly I saw the barrel of a rifle pointed at me. The face of the man who was pointing it peered from behind a tree with a malicious grin. I felt that death was near, and the feeling was not pleasant. However, the situation had an element of absurdity in it, and that made me laugh a little. The man who was going to kill me laughed too. I heard a little click, a report, and his gun went up, and he went down. Tom had shot him.

"Tom," said I, with some feeling, "you have saved my life."

"There!" said he, triumphantly, "you spoke first."

I saw that I had, and I was dreadfully provoked. However, he admitted that he was wrong; and so, under the circumstances, I decided that a reconciliation was advisable.

THE PROFESSOR HAS BEEN HERE today. He is the most delightful companion I know; and, what is his special charm, he really believes that he is hard and cynical, the tender-hearted old baby! I know that he fancies himself a second Diogenes. His liking for us boys is very queer to me. Tom is his pet, but he prefers to talk to me. He discusses Tom with me, and then he discusses me, just as if I were a third person. Today he told me I was a mass of selfish pettinesses. I don't think that was his word, but that was what he meant; "and yet," said he, "you are capable of heroic generosity." I always know that part of what the Professor says is said in earnest; but I am never quite sure what part it is. He doesn't fatigue me, and doesn't excite me, and it is well for me that he is here; still, I am impatient to get back again. He has told me about Tom's staying with me, instead of going home. I don't know what to say about it; I don't know what to think. It makes me want to die for him; nothing else that I can do seems sufficient. When this war is over, I suppose Tom will marry and forget me. I never will go near his wife—I shall hate her. Now, that is a very silly thing for a lieutenant-colonel to write. I don't care, it is true.

I WONDER IF I AM so very selfish, after all. I like refinement and elegance, and I hate dirt; and I do like to have people care for me and do things to oblige me. But my first thought is not always of myself; and I don't think I am unjust to others, because of myself. And, if I desire the sympathy and appreciation of others, I am sure it is not wrong.

"C'est qu'un cœur bien atteint veut qu'on soit tout à lui."

I can't remember, though, just now, a single unselfish thing that I have ever done, unless it was giving some of the fruit and jelly that the Professor brought me yesterday to a poor fellow with hungry eyes, whom I saw glaring at them through the door. That wouldn't have been generous, either, if he hadn't been a rebel. Giving aid and comfort to the enemy is the only generous action that I can discover of mine, after all myself-analysis. Confound self-analysis, anyway! It is only another form of selfishness, mingled with morbid conceit. If I did what I ought to do, without thinking about myself at all, it would be better for me; but I haven't anything to do just now, except scribble away here, and it is dreadfully stupid.

How talking with the Professor has set me to thinking of Harvard again! Now that the lights are glimmering at intervals through the ward, I can see the yard, with Holworthy and Stoughton and Hollis beaming away from their windows at each other, and Massachusetts standing a little apart, as becomes its greater age, but benignant in its seclusion. I hear the voices of singing in the yard, on the steps, and under the trees; I can see fellows sitting round the tables in their rooms, studying and not studying; I can hear recitations made to the different professors and tutors; and just as the bell for morning prayers, which I still hate, begins to clang upon my memory, I remember that I am here in a hospital, while we are still fighting and killing each other for the sake of the country that has given us all we enjoy. I shall be out soon, I know. There is always good prospect of a battle when I feel this way; and yet I do horribly loathe the tint of blood which has seemed to rest on everything I have seen or dreamed of for a year past. How I hate war, and yet how wholly I am absorbed in it! I am getting feverish; I shall write no more today.

In looking over my note-book, I find something which, luckily for me, I had almost forgotten; and that is, the prediction of my friend Mooney. Poor idiot! he was shot the first time that we were under fire. How pleasant it would have been for me in all the work I have been through, if I had remembered that prophecy! How it would have aided my recovery in my sickness, if I had been haunted by those words! I am to meet a dishonorable death for a dishonorable action, am I? The only dishonorable action I can commit is to go over to Stonewall Jackson, and learn how to fight. By Jove! I do admire that man. He is what too few officers on either the Union or the Rebel sides are, unselfish and in earnest. But I don't think that I shall join him, for all that; and, if I did, I should not be likely to meet with death,—his luck and his pluck would take me through.

The Professor has confided to me a plan of his, which delights me. He says that he will go North, and bring Tom's mother on to Washington, if her health permits. As Tom's father is in Europe at present, and as it would be highly unpleasant, to use the mildest term, for a lady to travel alone to Washington, knowing nothing of the place and its peculiarities, it is very thoughtful and very kind, and something more, in the Professor to do this. Then Tom can run up to Washington for a day or two to see her, poor fellow! and all, or rather part, of his great generosity will be rewarded. The Professor is a brick to think of it; and I have made him promise to start tomorrow. And when he goes, I shall go too, only in the other direction. How happy this will make Tom!

I DON'T KNOW WHAT MAKES me think of our class-day now, but I do wonder who had the rooms which Tom and I engaged for our spread. Perhaps it's the contrast between salad and strawberries, and hardtack and corned-beef; though now everything seems to me to be saturated with gruel. I wonder if Tiny Snow was at class-day this year! She was an object of awe to me in Freshman year; then I despised the sex when I was a Sophomore; and then in Junior year I saw a good deal of her. She had a way of drooping her head a little; and then, with a sort of shy little gulp, raising it, and making her eyes childlike and plaintive. It was quite pleasant, even after familiarity with it had destroyed its novelty. I wrote some verses to her once, and sent them to "The Harvard Magazine"; but they came into the hands of an editor who was gone on her himself, and he very properly rejected them. Once I showed Tiny, quite by accident, the Etruscan locket which I got abroad, and which Tom admired so much that I had his initials cut on it to give to him.

"Oh, how lovely!" said Tiny. "Who is it for?"

"Don't you see the initials?" said I

"T. S.," said she, innocently; "who can it be?"

I thought there seemed something like a blush upon her cheek as she spoke; but I told her that T. S. was someone I cared a great deal about.

"Is she pretty?" asked Tiny.

"She!" I answered; "it isn't any girl; it's my chum, Tom, you know."

Then she really colored; and a little while afterward I remembered that those were her initials. How she must have hated me,—perhaps!

I HAVE EATEN A REAL breakfast at last, and am upon my feet again. The Professor has gone, and I am going at once. How curious it will be to come out of this dream, and go back again to work! The doctor begs me not to get excited, and yet tells me that in three days I shall be as well as ever. I have been excited for a year now, and I go to the front this very afternoon. I am rather thin, and my shirt feels something like an air-box; but I shall get over all that soon. We are to make an attack before long, I understand.

　　　　　　　　　　　　　　　FREDERICK W. LORING

I AM BACK IN CAMP. This is the last entry that I shall make in this note-book for sometime to come. I am alarmed a little about Tom. I think he is going to be sick; he seems excited and feverish, and yet dull. However, he has brightened up wonderfully since I told him about the Professor's intention; and I am not sure but that it was a dreadful homesickness that oppressed him when I first met him. He won't see a doctor; he laughs the idea to scorn, and says he is only tired and overworked, and that, if I can manage to secure him a little rest, he will soon be all right. But he is dying to see his mother, he confesses to me, and I am not surprised to hear it.

I said that this is the last entry I shall make here. I am not sure now but that these are the last words which I shall ever write. I take charge of a small expedition tonight, with men whom I have personally selected for the purpose; and we are to destroy the bridge above here. It must be done at once. Jackson is near there, and we expect and fear an attack from him. The work is delicate rather than difficult; but it is sufficiently dangerous for me to commend my soul to God before I start upon it. Goodbye, little note-book, perhaps forever. If Tom and I return safe,—and Tom will, I am sure,—why, then, perhaps, I may tell you all about this coming night's work; but, if not, you will be destroyed, unread; and so farewell.

VIII

Midnight

"Then came a blinding flash, a deafening roar,
And dissonant cries of terror and dismay;
Blood trickled down the river's reedy shore,
And with the dead he lay."

A starlit sky, dead silence all around, only the river's murmur breaking it. The moonbeams shining on the forest-path mark all the shadows with a dazzling light, bringing weird and fantastic outlines forth, where brush and hedges line the dusty road, and making the parched fields, almost destitute of vegetation, shine like burnished sheets of dead white light. And along this road came slowly, with muffled tramp, a little body of men, their dark figures darker by contrast with the gleaming barrels of their rifles, which the moonlight seemed to tinge with silvery fire. They came along so quietly, so noiselessly, now hidden from view in a curve of the road, and now appearing again. And still all was quiet.

And then a little tongue of flame ran quickly and noiselessly up into the black darkness; and in a moment more all was blaze and smoke. The work was done,—the bridge was destroyed.

Down in the road around the bridge the men were grouped,—the fire giving them a ruddy coloring,—a tint of blood. Two figures were especially prominent, and seemed to be directing their movements.

"Well, Tom," said Ned, "does this remind you of bonfires in the yard at Cambridge?"

"Not much," said Tom, dispiritedly.

"Why, Tom, what is the matter with you?" asked Ned, anxiously.

"I don't know," said Tom. "I feel nervous and apprehensive."

"I ought not to have let you come with me," said Ned. "It was weak and selfish in me to consent. You are feverish and excited, Tom; and you ought to have rested."

"Just as if I was going to let you go off into danger without me!" said Tom.

"I am much obliged to you for the care you take of me," said Ned; "but you see the work has been done without any trouble. The rebs are two miles away; and this will prevent them from making a detour, and getting in our rear if we advance."

"Ned," said Tom, "do you think that the Professor will bring my mother on to Washington with him?"

"Think!" said Ned. "I am sure he will, and that, when we return to camp, we shall find a message from her to you. Perhaps he'll charter a train, and bring on a host of your female admirers, victorious masher of female hearts!"

"Don't rough me, Ned," said Tom.

"Well, now I know that you are going to be sick, Tom," said Ned, "when you take that piteous tone, instead of answering me back. By Jove, there goes a beam, crash; and look, the fire has entirely died out of the other. We can't leave the work half done in this way, we must hurry and finish it. The rebel pickets are probably back in camp by this time. Tom, order four men, and row that boat over to the other side for me."

"Why, Ned!" asked Tom, "what are you going to do?"

"The fire has died out over there," said Ned, "and the other beam is left. Here, O'Brien, I want that axe. I am going to cross on it, and cut it off where it is charred. Get the boat ready at once, captain."

"But, Ned, that is very dangerous," interposed Tom.

"Obey orders!" said Ned, impatiently and angrily; and Tom, with a reproachful glance, left him at once.

Only a slender beam now hung over the flood. On this Ned started to cross, balancing himself with the axe, the group of men watching him eagerly. An inch to the right or to the left, and all was lost. The flames were decreasing now, yet still the beam stood. Then the boat started out slowly across the river. The attention of all was turned towards it for an instant; and, in the mean time, Ned had almost gained the other side. One, two, three blows on the charred part of the beam, and it wavered and fell with a crash as Ned leaped lightly upon the bank. He waved his hand triumphantly, and ran down to meet the boat, which, more than half way across, was now struggling with the powerful current, and yet was visibly nearing the shore. He waved his cap, and started down the river-bank into the copse to meet it. Only two steps, two little steps down the bank, and from the tangled foliage a powerful hand grasped his throat, the cold barrel of a pistol was pressed to his cheek, and a voice fairly hissed the whisper into his ears:—

"Silence! or you are a dead man!"

And for reply, with one mighty effort, he threw off the hand; and, as the pistol-shot resounded through the air, his voice rang out, clear and strong on the still night:—

"Back to the Camp, For Your Lives!
The Enemy is Upon Us!"

In an instant more he was seized; and one of the men who had crept upon him said:—

"Damn you, you hound! you have spoiled all our plans."

Then Ned smiled serenely, and looked calmly at the man.

"But we shall bag four or five of them, anyway, lieutenant," said one of the men,—"those in the boat down there."

And then Ned started and turned pale; but it was too late. Tom and two others had already landed, and were in the hands of two or three of the rebel pickets.

"O Tom, Tom!" cried Ned, "why did you not turn back?"

But Tom did not answer, and only stared vacantly and stupidly at Ned.

"The captain's sick, sir," said one of the men who had been captured.

"Drunk, more likely," said the rebel lieutenant, with an oath.

"He was taken in the boat," continued the man.

"It is as I feared," said Ned; "he is in a high fever, as I was." At this the rebel lieutenant drew back. "Oh! it is not contagious," said Ned, with a world of scorn in his voice; and the rebel lieutenant resumed his former position.

"Tom, don't you know me?" asked Ned. "Oh, what will be the end of this, I wonder!"

"Libby Prison," sneered the lieutenant.

"Tell my mother to come and see me at Libby," said Tom, half stupidly. Upon this the chorus naturally raised an insulting shout, and one poor brute indulged in some ribald remark. In an instant, Tom had struck him across the face; in another instant, Tom himself lay on the ground senseless and stunned by a blow from the butt of one of the rebel rifles. It was at this instant, while Ned in anguish and desperation was struggling with his captors, that the sound of horses' hoofs was heard coming nearer and nearer, and three or four officers rode quickly up. The central figure of the group was a compact, sinewy man, of medium height, with a full, untrimmed beard, and a face, as Ned could see by the dim light of the fire which some of the men were now lighting a little distance off, furrowed with the lines of thought, of care, and anxiety. The eyes were large and expressive, the features clearly cut, and the mouth, even though partially hidden by a thin mustache, showed indomitable firmness. A grand head in many respects, and one which made it evident to Ned that he was in the presence of the dreaded Stonewall Jackson.

"What is the matter here?" he asked briefly.

"They have destroyed the bridge, general," was the reply.

Stonewall Jackson turned, and whispered to one of his companions who rode away. Then he continued:—

"Are these prisoners?"

"Yes, general," said the lieutenant,—"these four."

"A lieutenant-colonel, I see?" said Stonewall Jackson.

Ned simply bowed in reply. Then Stonewall Jackson looked at Tom, and said:—

"And who is this here?"

At this, Tom half raised himself, and then fell back again.

"May I tell you?" asked Ned.

"Certainly," said Jackson; "what is it?"

"He is in a high fever, which has been coming on for sometime," said Ned; "and one of these men struck him with the butt of his rifle."

"After he had surrendered?" asked Jackson.

"After he was taken prisoner," said Ned.

"He shall be taken to camp and attended to," said Stonewall Jackson. But, when they touched Tom, he uttered a sharp cry of pain; and the men drew back.

"We will let him remain here, then," said Jackson, after a word or two more with his companions. "Lieutenant, you will keep watch here, and down the river's bank, until daybreak, and then report at head-quarters to me with the prisoners. As for you, sir," he continued, addressing Ned, "you can remain here through the night with your friend,—under parole, of course, not to break your bonds. Do you accept?"

"Most thankfully," said Ned, with a gratitude in his voice and accent far beyond what his words expressed.

"He is a handsome boy," said Jackson, looking again at the still unconscious Tom. "Keep the other prisoners under strict guard, lieutenant; but treat this gentleman who is under parole with all possible respect. Hark! what is that? Midnight!"

And, as he paused to listen, the distant sound of bells rang faintly out upon the air. Midnight; and for an instant utter stillness upon air and earth and water. And then Tom groaned painfully; and, as Ned bent anxiously over him, Stonewall Jackson said:—

"I shall see you in the morning, Colonel." And Ned thanked him once again; and the noise of the horses' hoofs came more and more faintly, and at last died away entirely.

Then Ned knelt down beside Tom, and looked steadily at him. Tom half opened his eyes, and then closed them again with a weary moan that went to Ned's very heart. "Don't you know me, Tom?" he said.

"I shall see my mother tomorrow," said Tom, "after waiting two years. I couldn't go before,—I couldn't leave Ned when he was sick."

Ned hid his face in his hands, and groaned. Tom closed his eyes again, and seemed to pass into a fitful slumber. The men had built a great fire a little way apart; and its gleams fell upon Tom's face, just as the firelight had done in the Professor's room, five years before, when Ned first met him. How well he remembered that night! He laid his hand on Tom's hot brow, and smoothed back his tangled hair. How lovely his face was in this fitful, ruddy glow! How much he had sacrificed for Ned, and now Ned had ruined him! It was dreadful to Ned. He threw himself on the grass beside Tom, and put his face on Tom's shoulder.

"I am going to cut recitation today," muttered Tom. "Hang that old Ned! He is always vexed about something or other. I'm going to enlist, mother; I must, you see,—oh, I must, I must, I must! Goodbye!"

"Oh, don't, Tom!" groaned Ned.

And then Tom sat up, and gazed wildly and vacantly at Ned, without a trace of recognition in his face.

"Why, Professor," said he. "I couldn't leave Ned possibly! We've been through everything together; and he might not be cared for properly, if I were to leave him sick and alone. Mother says that I am right; and I shall see her tomorrow,—I shall see her tomorrow."

"It is as I feared," said Ned, half to himself; "he is in a high fever. If I can only get him down to the river-bank there, where I can bathe his head."

And, putting Tom's limp arm around his own neck, Ned managed with some difficulty to carry him a few steps to the river's brink.

"There, Tom," he said, "I'll bathe your head for you, poor fellow!"

"Here is the river," said Tom; "and we are going to see mother in a boat. It's a dangerous thing, Ned, to cross on that beam. OBEY ORDERS! And now it is too late, too late! God only knows whether I shall ever see my mother again." And now, as Tom became quiet once more, Ned sat there, and bathed his head; and the river continued the noise of its rushing waters, and the wavelets splashed gently upon the shore, and against the wooden sides of the boat,—the boat! And now for the first time Ned saw the means of deliverance within his power. The idea fairly swept over his mind. To put Tom into the boat, and gain the other side, would be the work of a few moments only: and it could be done; for the rebel squad was dispersed along the shore, and the one man who sat by the fire a few yards off seemed fast asleep. But then, even as the thought of a possibility of freedom for Tom made him exultant, there came the recollection of his parole. He still sat by Tom's side, and mechanically now smoothed back the hair from his forehead, and as mechanically repeated to himself, "word of honor, word of honor, word of honor," until the very leaves upon the trees seemed to rustle in rhythm with the cadence; and then, with this dull, heavy oppression on his mind, the words seemed to turn into French and Latin and Greek, and to make new and fantastic combinations in his brain. "God help me!" he groaned. "I am going mad." And then he knelt and prayed; and still the river rushed along, and still that one black figure sat there by the fire, as if half asleep. Then Ned saw him move slowly, and heard him whisper hoarsely, "Colonel! Colonel!"

"Do you mean me?" asked Ned.

"Yes. Speak softer, and come up here."

Wondering and confused, Ned obeyed. The man turned a rough, unshaven face to him, and said:—

"You don't know me, I see?"

"No," said Ned.

"I know you, though. Mighty peart you be now; but you wasn't so three weeks ago. You was took pretty sick then, and lying in a hospittle."

"Well, what of it?" said Ned.

"Well, you're a stoutish kind of man now, ain't you? But, Lord!" and the fellow laughed to himself, "I could just chaw you up in no time. I should kinder like to have a gouge at you, anyway."

"Thank you," said Ned; "but if that is all you have to say, I shall have to leave you, and attend to my friend."

"You're a real perlite man," said the man, in a wondering sort of way; "and yet you're a Yank. You must attend to your friend. That's fair; and why? Because when you was sick, he took care of you. I see it; I was in the hospittle likewise at the time. I had just got up as you was took down. Don't yer remember me?"

"No," said Ned, impatiently.

"Well, you give me some fruit and jelly that was sent me one day. I never had such a good time in my life as eating them things. The nurse, she says, 'Don't waste 'em on him; he's a rebel,' she says; and what did you say? You says, 'Don't let's think nothing about Rebs and Feds here,' says you, 'but let's forget all about it; and then I liked you. I like you now.'"

"I am glad to hear it," said Ned; "but I must see to my friend."

"You care for him about as you would for a gal, don't you?" said this Virginia barbarian then. "Well, he's pootier than any gal I ever see anywhar. Look here, this is jest what I want to say to you. Ef you should put him and you in that thar boat, and float down the river, you'd come to your own lines. Ef I should see you do it, I'd stop you; but I'm going to take a snooze by the fire here, for I'm powerful tired. Ef I should wake up, I should fire on you, ef I saw you; and so would others. But I can't allus aim straight in the dark; and, whar one aims, others is likely to. Now I have done you a good turn for what you've did to me; and ef ever we meet again, by God, I'll kill you."

"But I can't in honor escape," said Ned.

"Of course you can't," said the man; "and, if you could, of course you wouldn't tell me. There, I don't want no more to say to you. Just git, that's all you've got to do."

Ned went back full of this new temptation. The other pickets were dispersed, the river rolled on invitingly, and Tom seemed to be sleeping more quietly than before.

"Perhaps I can get him exchanged in the morning," said Ned, "since he's so ill. I am glad that he is sleeping."

Just at this moment, Tom awoke hurriedly, and looked about him wildly and vacantly, then fell back again.

"Oh, if Ned were only here!" he groaned,—"if Ned were only here!"

"Ned is here, Tom, close beside you, as always," said Ned, softly.

"If Ned were here," muttered Tom, "he would help me. O Ned, Ned! do come, do please come and help me to see my mother!"

"I will," whispered Ned, solemnly. Not an instant was to be lost. Without daring to think, without daring to look around him, then he lifted Tom and laid him in the boat. The keel grated on the pebbly shore. He started nervously and turned; but the faithless picket was laboriously sleeping. In an instant more he had thrown off his outer garments; and, with the rope of the boat tied around his neck, he half swam, half drifted, with the strong current down the stream. Weak from his late

FREDERICK W. LORING

sickness, and the excitement and efforts of the night, his swimming soon exhausted him; and he clung to the side of the boat, and drifted with it. The sky now was marked with black cloud-rifts, that made strange and fantastic outlines on its luminous background; and the white light of the moon was growing gray. On each side of him he saw the black trees standing in groups, now dense, now scattered, along the shores; while ever in his ears was the strange murmur of the torrent, broken only by Tom's incoherent muttering as he lay in the boat. Then suddenly came the sharp report of a rifle; and he knew that his escape was discovered at last. He heard the bullets whistle by him, then one grazed the side of the boat, but luckily did not come near Tom. At last the firing ceased; but the boat seemed to be drifting into a little cove. He made one desperate effort to push her more into the main current, but in vain; for his strength was now entirely gone. Then he gave one cry, as he saw the first faint gleam of dawn in the east, and the boat struck him, bruised and fainting, against the shore. He crawled feebly upon the bank, the rope still around his neck; and then, stunned and bruised, all consciousness forsook him. The last thing which he knew was, that the birds were just beginning to twitter in the trees.

WHEN HE AWOKE IT WAS later in the day; and the warm light and air of the forenoon was streaming into his tent. An orderly was standing by the entrance.

"Where is Tom?" he asked hoarsely.

"The captain is there"; and the orderly pointed to the other side of the tent, where Ned saw a figure lying muffled in coats and blankets. He hardly dared to ask what he dreaded to learn, his voice seemed clogged and heavy in his throat; and finally, when he did speak, it was in a hoarse and tremulous whisper:—

"Is he dead?"

"Dead?" said the orderly, surprised; "why, no, colonel! But he is dreadfully sick; and they are going to take him to the hospital, after you have seen him and spoken with him."

"Go outside," said Ned, briefly, "and let no one enter under any pretext whatever." And, as the orderly obeyed, he threw himself down beside Tom, who was sleeping restlessly under the influence apparently of some opiate.

He looked at him, laid his hand upon his forehead, and then bent over and kissed his hot face.

"Tom," he said. But there was no answer, no movement. "I have come to bid you goodbye, Tom," he said; "I am going back to deliver myself up." But still Tom slept, and groaned.

"Not one word of goodbye, Tom," said poor Ned. "And yet this is the last time—the very last time—God help me!—that we shall see each other, that I shall see you. O my darling, my darling, my darling! please hear me. The only one I have ever loved at all, the only one who has ever loved me. The last words that you heard from me were those of anger and impatience, and now, poor fellow! you cannot speak even to say goodbye. Hear me say it. When you get well again, have some memory of my bending over you and saying it, and telling you that I was saying goodbye, goodbye, goodbye! O Tom, my darling! don't forget it. If you knew how I love you, how I have loved you in all my jealous, morbid moods, in all my exacting selfishness,—O Tom! my darling, my darling! can't you say one word, one little word before we part,—just one little word, if it were only my name? Oh, please, please speak to me! Don't you remember when we were examined for college together? You sat across the hall. I saw you there; and I wanted to go over and help you. And your picture, Tom, that we quarrelled about,—I have it now, Tom; it will be with me when they bury me. Tom, don't you remember that picture? It was the night when I determined to go to war that you gave me that picture; it was just before we enlisted. O Tom! why did I let you come at all? You will see your mother, Tom; and you will go home now, and marry, and be happy, and forget me. Oh, no, no, no, Tom! you won't do that; you can't do that. You won't forget Ned, darling; he was something to you; and you were all the world to him. O Tom! Tom! please say one word to him." He stopped and was silent. Tom only moaned restlessly in his sleep; and there seemed to be a painful death-like silence inside the tent, while outside was the bright life of the morning and the busy murmur of the camp.

"Ah, well!" he said, "it is better so. He would not let me go if he were conscious; he would say that I must stay with him; and that cannot be. He need not know that I am dead, as I shall be, until he himself is well once again. Goodbye, Tom! goodbye! and God bless you forever, my darling!"

And calmly, yet with a dreadful pang at his heart, he stooped, and once more kissed the flushed face of his friend; then quickly, as if impelled by some force not his own, without daring to look backward, he rushed from the tent.

FREDERICK W. LORING

IX

The Beginning of the End

"The morn broke in upon his solemn dream;
And still with steady pulse and deepening eye,
'Where bugles call,' he said, 'and rifles gleam,
I follow though I die.'"

Stonewall Jackson sat in his tent, writing rapidly on a rough pine table. There was in the man, in spite of his old coat stained here and there with mud, and his awkwardness of position and figure, an appearance of power,—power conscious and self-sustaining. At a first glance he seemed an old Virginia farmer; but an instant's careful scrutiny showed, beneath his awkward simplicity, the grace of a true soldier, while the slow, hesitating speech had in it an undertone which made it evident that at times each word might be charged with fire and eloquence and life. As he moved one hand to brush back the thinned hair on his temples, this hot afternoon, a staff-officer entered the tent.

"I have some curious news, General," he said.

"What is it?" asked Jackson, briefly; for a word was a power with this man, and he never wasted power.

"The prisoner who broke his parole this morning has returned here," said the officer.

"What!" exclaimed Jackson, "has he given himself up?"

"Yes, General; they have him in confinement, and he has asked to see you."

"To see me, lieutenant!" said Stonewall Jackson. "That will make no difference. He is to be shot at sunrise."

"Very well, General"; and the lieutenant turned to depart.

"Stop a moment, though," said Jackson. "I should like to know what defence, what excuse he has to offer. Have him brought here."

"Very well, General. But he is to be shot?"

"Certainly, sir!"

Jackson laid down his pen, and folded his arms before him on the rough board which served him as a writing-table. He had not long to wait. In less than five minutes, Ned appeared, guarded by two soldiers, his face pale but determined. He met Stonewall Jackson's scrutinizing look clearly and fearlessly, yet respectfully. "You may withdraw," said Jackson to the men. "Now, sir, you wish to see me. What have you to say?"

"I broke my parole this morning," said Ned.

"I know it, sir," said Jackson; "and, having some compunction for your violation of honor, you have tried as a manœuvre giving yourself up again. You have made a mistake, sir."

"It is just because I knew you would misconstrue my motive and my action thus that I asked to see you," said Ned. "I wish to explain."

"No explanation is possible, sir," cried Stonewall Jackson; "and this will avail you nothing."

"Oh! wait a moment," cried Ned, impetuously. "Don't deceive yourself. I know what I am doing; I knew a few hours ago, when I left the Union lines, what I was doing. I came here to die,—to be shot! Do you hear,—to be shot! I broke my parole; I expected no mercy from you,—I ask for none, I would take none. I claim only my right, and my right is death."

"Then why did you give yourself up, if you knew death must be your fate?" asked Jackson.

"Death has not frightened me very much," said Ned, contemptuously.

"There is something about you," said Stonewall Jackson, "which makes me wish to respect you. I see you are not a coward."

"And I wish you to see that I am not a liar," answered Ned. "I gave myself up to death; and I wish you to bear witness, that, having sinned, I accepted the penalty."

"But why sin?" said Stonewall Jackson.

"I will tell you why," said Ned. "I have only one person in the world to care for: I have no family, no relatives, only this one friend. He was all the world to me, and I was something to him. When the war broke out, I enlisted, and he went with me. We have been side by side through everything. He saved my life in battle at the risk of his own; and a few weeks ago, when I was taken sick by fever, and he had a leave of absence, he gave up his home, he sacrificed everything, to watch by me. Last night he was taken sick while with the party at the bridge, when in another day he would have been with his mother at Washington. You paroled me. I was left there with him, and he raved and groaned until I could bear it no longer. Every word he said seemed to stab me to the heart. Then I saw the river and the boat; the men were scattered, and the means of escape were at hand. I hesitated. I thought of my parole;

and then I thought of him a prisoner, an invalid, a corpse perhaps, if he waited here, while back of us his mother was hastening to meet her only son. He had given up so much for me, and what had I done for him? It seemed as if I must get him away; and then he cried out again, 'Ned, Ned, won't you help me?' And I said, 'Yes!' And I knew that *yes* was death to me. Oh! you see I am prepared. I have not tried to arouse your sympathy or your compassion, I have only told you the bare facts. Do you think, if I hoped for life, if I cared for pardon from you, that I could not say more, that I could not pour out words of fire and blood to show you what our friendship is, and what last night's temptation was? I ask no mercy; and you could give me none if you wished it: my act must bring its consequences. Only I wished you to see that I was neither liar nor coward; that, having forfeited my life, I did not evade the payment of my debt; in a word, that I was enough of a gentleman to be worthy of the great privilege of serving in my country's cause."

"Sir," said Jackson, "you are not only a gentleman, but a soldier. I love war for itself, I glory in it; but it saddens me when it brings with it the useless sacrifice of such a life as yours."

"I am not a soldier," said Ned, quietly. "I hate war; I hate to have to long for the death of such a man as you are. But I am ready for all that, when there is a cause at stake."

"A cause at stake!" said Stonewall Jackson. "Well, God be with the right!"

"God is with the right," said Ned; "and time will show us which is the right. Ah! if I could live to see that time!"

"Be thankful rather," said Jackson, "that you are going to die before you find you are in the wrong. I wish you had been with me in this campaign."

"If it had been possible," said Ned, and then he stopped.

"I should like," said Stonewall Jackson, slowly, "though doubtless you consider me a rebel and a traitor, to have you shake hands with me."

"Not with a rebel or a traitor," said Ned, "but with a sincere and honest man whom I respect and honor"; and with this grasp of hands, these two great souls gazed in each other's eyes.

"And now you know what I must say," said Stonewall Jackson.

"I know it," Ned replied.

"Do not think me cruel, do not think me lacking in human feeling," Stonewall Jackson continued; "but war has its duties as well as peace. God help those who must execute these duties!"

"There is but one thing you can do," said Ned, tranquilly.

"There is but one thing I can do," repeated Jackson. "You will be shot at sunrise." He called the men outside. "Give this gentleman," he said, "as good accommodations as the camp affords. See that he is left by himself, and is undisturbed tonight.—All letters, all directions, which you may wish to give, shall be forwarded to the North," he continued, addressing Ned; "and if you wish anything to be done about burial"—

"I shall wish nothing," said Ned.

"In that case," said Jackson, with princely courtesy, "I have only to say farewell." He rose again, and took Ned's hand; then the soldiers marched away, and he was left in his tent alone.

X

The Last Letter Home

Dear Professor,

I am writing to you the last words I shall ever say, the last thoughts I shall ever think, the last farewell to all I have ever known and loved. Tomorrow, at daybreak, I am to be shot. There is nothing that can possibly prevent it,—this is my last night on earth. Am I resigned to my lot? am I willing to lose my life? I cannot tell, it seems so like a dream. It is terrible to me to think that this is the end of all my youth and hope; and you will understand me when I say that I do dread and fear death. Yet I am calm and self-possessed. I am half dead already, indeed, for my end seems inevitable; and I do not suffer so much as I wonder. I seem to have lost all volition, and, as it were, to have gone out of myself. A little while ago I wound up my watch; and then the uselessness of that performance struck me, and I said, half aloud, "Poor Ned!" and then laughed at myself for doing it. As my laugh died away, there was a cold silence around which chilled me through and through. Yes, I must be half dead already. It is only when I think of Tom that the life seems to rush back again; and as I believe this sort of torpor is well for me, I dare not trust to myself write to him. Besides, he must get well; and so you must try and keep my death hidden from him for a time. You can tell him, better than I could, that my last thought will be of him, and that I cannot trust myself to say farewell to him. Even now, I have this cruel uncertainty about his health, and I do not know but what you may lose us both.

Stonewall Jackson is a hero. I never thought that I could say that of any rebel, but I am glad that I have known him. He will work us more terrible injury, I fear; but I am sure that he will not live long. The excitement of this war is killing him; and here, when I so thoroughly admire him, I have to rejoice that he is doomed. How strange war is,—stranger and stranger now than ever! Oh! if I could only see the end,—if I could only know whether we shall gain our country by all this blood, and if Tom will live, I could die perfectly contented. There is Tom again, you see. I have to think of him in spite of myself. When you tell him my story, you can give him this letter, if he wants it, as perhaps he will.

And now goodbye for yourself. It is not well for me to write,—it brings me back to life too much; but I cannot die without telling you something of my feeling for you. Do you think that I have not fully appreciated all your sympathy, all your kindness, all the wealth of intellect and culture which you have laid before me? I always have had a sort of hope, that sometime, when I should win some great honor, and the world should applaud, I could say, "Look here; here is the man to whom I owe all this; here is the man who advised me, who guided me; the man with the strong soul and the woman's tenderness, who loved youth and beauty, and sympathized with sorrow. You take off your hats to me; but I kneel before him." But all that is over now, and you have only a numb goodbye from a man who is to be shot in a few hours.

My body will not be sent North. When I am dead, I am dead; and here or there, it matters not where it is buried, to me nor to anyone else. But if you ever want to think of me, and to feel that I am near, walk through the yard at Harvard, over by Holworthy, in the lovely evenings of the spring weather. It was at such a season, and at such a time, that I last saw the dear old place; and, if I ever can be anywhere on earth again, it is there that I should choose to be. Ah, if I could only see Harvard once again! God bless it forever and forever! I wonder how many visions of its elm-trees have swept before dying eyes here in Virginia battle-fields!

Ah, well! there is only goodbye to say once more. When he asks for me, tell him that I constantly think of him, that I am well and happy. Don't let him know the truth until he is clearly out of danger, and then tell him all. It is not so very hard to bear; and I am sure now that I shall never be forgotten by him, and that nothing can ever come between us now. Tell him the only thing, after God, worth living for and worth dying for, is our country,—our noble country. Oh! she must be strong and glorious and united, at any cost. I feel it and I know it. And now goodbye, once more and forever.

He sealed and directed the letter; then, throwing himself on the blanket in the corner of the tent, fell into a deep, refreshing slumber. He woke to feel the grasp of a hand upon his shoulder, to see a file of men beside him. Without a word he rose and went with them. They led him out a little from the camp, where it seemed quiet. He saw them stand before him; he heard one preliminary order given, and caught the flash of rifle-barrels in the early morning sunlight. Then there was a noise and disturbance in the camp beyond, and a voice cried out:—

"It's an attack by the Federals!"

Ned turned involuntarily. And with these words, in one great sweeping flood, his life came back. No more numbness, no more indifference; but, in that one instant, every drop of blood in his veins seemed charged with electric power, and the morning air was like nectar. He stood there, strong, like a man; and then there was one report, and he fell dead,—dead in the dust of the Virginia soil.

XI

Afterwards

This is the one picture that has been ever before my eyes, even in the wild regions of Nevada and the undulating lawns and woody slopes of California. In the snow-clad forests of the Sierra Nevada, and even in the tropical glory of sky and air in Arizona, amid the noise and bustle of the camp, with heavenly peace and loveliness above, and murderous savages, thirsting for our blood lying in deadly ambush all around, I still have seen this picture. A dead man lying with his face to the earth; while close by his side one little spot of dust seems blackened and congealed by blood.

And afterwards? The sunshine steals softly and furtively through the darkened windows of a happy Northern home. It is June, and the perfume of the roses is on the air. In an easy-chair half sits, half reclines, a pale girl, with a happy face, looking down with a perfect smile at Tom, who sits at her feet. And near by stands a nurse, holding in her arms a baby,—a baby whose two gelatinous arms beat the air wildly, while his voice is raised in a shrill note, which may be triumph or which may be agony.

"By Jove!" Tom says admiringly, "his high notes are stunning; ar'n't they, Nettie?"

"Tom," replies Nettie, threateningly, "dare to make fun of your offspring again, and we will leave you, and start for Indiana. Won't we, Baby?"

To this question, reply is given by an absurd inclination of the head on one side and another wheezy shriek.

"I am not laughing, I am not laughing," Tom hastens to remark, lest the threat of Indiana should be repeated; "so don't get angry, Baby. I say, Nettie, we must have a name for him. We can't call him Baby all the time, you know."

"He was named long ago, Tom," said Nettie, "though of course I had to wait. We must call him 'Ned;' we couldn't call him by any other name."

"Thank you, darling," said Tom, gravely; "that is the way you make me love you more and more everyday." And he kisses his wife, and, rising, takes the baby and looks on its face, while his eyes are filled with tears.

And afterwards? The Professor's room at Harvard is still as it was when we first knew it, with the photograph still hanging over the mantel-piece. And the Professor sits there gazing at it more lonely now than ever before. He is growing quite old; he is very sarcastic and astonishing; and dreadful stories are current among the students in regard to his severity against culprits in the meetings of the Faculty. There are two or three who know him, and to whom he is very kind. They heard him tell the story of his boys, and they heard poor Ned's last letter. But the Professor declared then that he should never speak of the subject again; and the few who heard him saw that the rest of his life must be sad. And now, as he takes up the notes and emendations of his old lecture on "Domestic Arts," whose turn has come again, his eye falls on the picture. Again it is the spring weather, again the fresh breeze enters his room. He rises and walks to the window.

"I wonder if he is near," he says, half aloud. "'It was in such a season and at such a time, that I last saw the dear old place; and, if ever I can be on earth again, it is there that I should wish to be.' Poor Ned! Poor Ned!"

And, as he sits in his chair again, the picture fades from my view, and I see only the moonlight on our mountain camp, and hear the wailing of the western wind.

And afterwards? Once more the country is intact, freed from the deadly perils which assailed her. We know now what the words "our country" mean,—rocks which the Atlantic lashes with its spray; broad uplands and vast prairies where almost spontaneously fruit and grain seem to spring forth from the rich soil; and barren hills as well, with only the sage-brush for vegetation, within whose secret treasure-houses lie great masses of gold and silver ore. From the summits of the Sierra Nevada you can stand at midsummer in a forest where wreaths of snow lie on the trees, and can gaze far down into valleys, thousands of feet beneath, where there are rippling streamlets, and masses of flowers of the most brilliant and the most delicate hues. This wonderful country, that is still in its infancy, that is nursing men of every nation to form a new nation; this country, that, with all its imperfections, stands now on the grand basis of universal freedom,—justifies not merely enthusiasm, but any loss of human life which may aid in its preservation. These friends, these brothers, knew what was the true meaning of life, and with that knowledge, gained by zeal and study, offered their lives as a sacrifice. Woe to our country should the great debt owed to these heroes be ever forgotten!

> *"May God forbid that yet,*
> *Or in all time to come, we should their names forget!*
> *May every spring-time's hours*
> *See their graves strewn with flowers,*
> *To show that still remembered is our debt!"*

A Note About the Author

Frederick W. Loring (1848–1871) was an American poet, novelist, and journalist. Born in Boston, he was a distant grandson of English settler Thomas Loring, who arrived in New England in 1634. Educated at Phillips Academy and Harvard University, Loring showed early promise as a writer and literary scholar, no doubt stemming from his late mother's encouragement and love of reading. After graduating from college, where he contributed to the *Harvard Advocate* literary magazine, Loring published a novel, *Two College Friends* (1871), and a poetry collection entitled *The Boston Dip and Other Verses* (1871). Over the next year, he found publication in such journals and periodicals as *The Atlantic Monthly, The Independent, Every Saturday,* and *Appleton's Journal.* For the latter, Loring left in spring of 1871 to report on the expedition of Lieutenant George M. Wheeler to Arizona. In November of that year, having passed through Death Valley at the height of summer and published several articles for *Appleton's,* Loring was among six stagecoach passengers killed in an attack by a group of Yavapai in the vicinity of Wickenburg Arizona. He is remembered today as a talented writer whose promising career was cut short before it could fully blossom. Loring's only novel has been praised as a pioneering story of male homosexuality for its depiction of young men united by friendship, romance, and tragedy.

A Note from the Publisher

Spanning many genres, from non-fiction essays to literature classics to children's books and lyric poetry, Mint Edition books showcase the master works of our time in a modern new package. The text is freshly typeset, is clean and easy to read, and features a new note about the author in each volume. Many books also include exclusive new introductory material. Every book boasts a striking new cover, which makes it as appropriate for collecting as it is for gift giving. Mint Edition books are only printed when a reader orders them, so natural resources are not wasted. We're proud that our books are never manufactured in excess and exist only in the exact quantity they need to be read and enjoyed.

Discover more of your favorite classics with Bookfinity™.

- Track your reading with custom book lists.
- Get great book recommendations for your personalized Reader Type.
- Add reviews for your favorite books.
- AND MUCH MORE!

Visit **bookfinity.com** and take the fun Reader Type quiz to get started.

Enjoy our classic and modern companion pairings!